Blazing Bert vs. Terraria
The Search for Cthulhu

By Joe Circles

Contents

Introduction

Somewhere, in the real world, someone playing Terraria creates a new character. They select the character's appearance at random, tufty bright red hair, a long red overcoat, peach coloured skin, blue trousers and white shoes.

When prompted to enter the character's name they type the first thing that comes to their head:

Blazing Bert

Chapter 1
Arrival

Bert opens his eyes for the first time, blinks and looks around. The world spread out before him is green and tree-lined. Far off in the distance he can make out the peaks of snowy white mountains and what appears to be huge red hills.

Bert knows a few things about himself and his surroundings, he is not sure how, he just does.

He is in the game Terraria.
He is a new character.
His name is Blazing Bert.
He has an inventory, his pack.

However the list of things Bert does not know worries him far more.

What does he do now?
Is he safe?

If he is not safe, how does he get to safety?

What is that moving in the hedge up ahead......

Without thinking, Bert reaches in his pack and pulls out his copper shortsword. Keeping low he moves slowly towards the rustling hedge, he catches sight of something moving within and raises his sword. A man jumps out and then almost falls backwards into the hedge again at the sight of Bert stood there, sword raised, ready to strike.

'Don't hurt me, please!' the man shouts in panic, crouching low, arms raised protectively over his head.

Bert lowers his sword and the man stands, brushing off a few stray leaves from his long brown coat and untangling a twig from his dusty brown hair. He reaches out a hand to shake with Bert's. Bert looks at the man and decides he does not look particularly dangerous. He shakes his hand.

'The name's Maxwell,' the man says, 'I'm the Guide.'

Chapter 2

Guidance

Bert is in the process of building a wooden hut, somewhere safe for them to stay ready for the arrival of night-time. Maxwell suggested this should be Bert's first job after he had explained the basics of mining, building, crafting and general survival.

Earlier, whilst Bert had been collecting wood and finding a spot to build a hut, Maxwell had explained each new world starts with a Guide whose job is to help the character through the game, especially in the early stages. When Bert had asked how he could get out of this world to safety, Maxwell had been unusually lost for words, eventually suggesting building the hut should be the priority and once that was done there would be time for more questions later.

Bert is nearly finished with the hut, despite not wanting to answer all of his questions Maxwell still manages to talk endlessly about a variety of other things from Antlions to Zombies. Bert does not mind, it makes the work go quicker listening to his chatter. However he occasionally looks up from his work and catches a glimpse of the Guide looking around nervously, a confused frown on his face, something is worrying him, something he does not seem to want to talk about.

Bert finishes crafting his first ever door; he is admiring his handy work when something catches his eye up ahead coming through the trees. The sun reflects off a green shiny surface and it is heading their way. Bert taps Maxwell on the arm, interrupting his story of how he had once seen a squirrel riding a Fallen Star.

'Is that anything we need to be worrying about?' Bert asks, pointing.

Maxwell looks up and squints to where Bert is indicating. 'Hmm, looks like a green slime, pretty much as weak as baddies get. Grab your sword and let's get rid of him. Looks like you're about to face your first enemy.'

Chapter 3
Fight

Bert pulls his copper shortsword from his pack and, with Maxwell close behind, makes his way towards the approaching enemy. As they get closer, Bert can see the slime in more detail. A green blob of see-through liquid; it is about half his own size and makes a wet squelchy slap each time it hits the ground.

'Only one of them, this should be easy enough.' Maxwell says, however, before he has even finished speaking, another two slimes jump out from behind the first. At the same moment they hear a noise behind them and turn to see three more slimes closing in.

'Oh, make that six.' Maxwell corrects himself, pulling a wooden bow out of his own pack, his expression turning serious for a change.

Bert slices at the closest slime, the sword makes a liquid noise as it hits the gooey surface, and after several more slashes the slime pops, defeated, leaving only a small puddle of goo on the ground. He hears the twanging noise of Maxwell's bow as the Guide fires arrow after arrow at the slimes approaching behind them. Bert concentrates on the next enemy in front. He slashes hard; knocking it back and giving him time to deal with the other one. He continues attacking until both slimes are dealt with.

'A little help please!' Maxwell calls from next to him.

Bert turns in time to see a slime jumping at the Guide. Without thinking, Bert pushes Maxwell out of the way and the slime lands on him instead. There is pain as the slime squashes him to the ground, however, it does not last long as it leaps off him readying for its next attack. Whilst it is still mid-jump, Bert gets to his feet and deals it enough blows to turn it into another puddle of goo.

Between them they make quick work of the remaining two slimes. Bert collects up the dropped slime, as advised by Maxwell, and the two head back to the hut. Bert's arms ache from swinging his sword so much and his back aches from where the slime landed on him. If that's the easiest enemy, he thinks to himself, I may be in trouble here.

Chapter 4

Problems

It has taken a while but the hut is complete and after a few more missions outside, thankfully without any more enemy encounters, Bert has a work bench, two chairs and a few torches, one of which he places in the hut to light it up. The hut is not big or comfy, but it is safe and for now it is home. He has also crafted himself some Wood armour, he thinks he looks rather silly wearing it and is worried about splinters, but he knows it is a good idea.

It is getting dark outside so Maxwell suggests they avoid going out again until day time, at least until Bert has a stronger weapon or some stronger armour, preferably both. As they sit waiting out the night, Maxwell is unusually quiet and avoids making eye contact with Bert.

'So what exactly is going on here?' Bert asks.

Maxwell fidgets in his chair before answering. 'Well, this is Terraria, I'm an NPC - a non-player character, the Guide. You're a character but, well, as you can see when you're not being played you can do what you want. That's about it really.' he says this then quickly looks away again.

'I know all that,' Bert says, 'but what I want to know is what's got you so worried, you don't seem the quiet type but all of a sudden you won't talk, or look at me. Also, you seemed surprised by how many slimes attacked us earlier.'

'Well....you see, I need to speak to the other guys, the other NPCs, before I can really say.' Maxwell says.

'Wait, you can speak to other NPCs, where are they?' Bert asks, looking around as if they might suddenly be in the room with them.

'Well yeah, we can all move around the different worlds as and when we want.'

'So, can I go and see the other NPCs?' Bert asks.

'Normally yes, at the moment, no. Characters like yourself, when the game is not being played, well they automatically go to the tutorial.' Maxwell replies.

'And I'm guessing this is not the tutorial?' Bert asks.

'No way, tutorials are safe. No baddies, no night time. Characters build themselves up nice cosy homes, they can leave and travel as they wish, but to be honest they don't normally. There's just no need for them to leave the safety of the tutorial for the dangers of the other worlds.'

'So why am I not in the tutorial with them?' Bert asks.

Maxwell shrugs, 'I honestly do not know. You should have automatically gone to the tutorial but you seem to be somehow stuck here...'

'What should I do then?' Bert asks, feeling helpless.

Maxwell smiles and pats him on the shoulder. 'Don't worry, we'll get you through the night, get some more supplies and then I'll head off for a bit to have a chat with some of the other NPCs and characters. Don't worry, between us we'll get you out of here to safety. Don't worry!'

He just said don't worry three times, Bert thinks, that cannot be a good sign.

Chapter 5

All Alone

Bert struggles to get to sleep that night, partly because sleeping in a wooden chair is uncomfortable, partly because every so often he hears strange noises outside. Maxwell had assured him it was just the Zombies and that having the work bench pushed up against the door meant they were not getting in. Regardless of the bench, Bert did not find it particularly reassuring to know there were Zombies roaming free right outside his door.

When he falls asleep Bert's dreams are strange, filled with images of giant flying eyeballs and floating brains. He is woken by the sound of shouting, Maxwell is yelling in his sleep.

'No, please, don't drop it in the lava, please. Not the wall, not the wall.'

Maxwell's bizarre sounding nightmare seems to pass and he quietens down again. Trying not to wake the Guide Bert gets up, opens the door a crack and peers out. The sun has risen and apart from a white bunny hopping in some long grass, he cannot see anything moving outside. Behind him he hears Maxwell wake with a loud yawn.

'I do not like sleeping in chairs,' Maxwell says through his yawn, 'we need beds, but that will take a bit of work. For now let's get you some more important survival gear before I head off.'

Having gone on another mission outside with Maxwell, thankfully only running into a few slimes, Bert now has a furnace and a small supply of mushrooms to help him recover any lost health. He also has a cosy looking campfire outside the hut and a few other basic, but useful, items which Maxwell helped him collect and craft.

Maxwell bids him farewell saying he will be back before nightfall, hopefully with some answers. He suggests if Bert goes anywhere to make sure it is always within sight of the hut and if he gets into any trouble, to just run in and shut the door. Maxwell smiles and waves but Bert can still see the worried look he is trying to hide. He then watches as one second the Guide is stood in front of him and the next, he has simply disappeared.

Bert suddenly feels very alone in this new and strange world.

Chapter 6
Day Zombies

To help pass the time Bert decides to go in search of some more supplies. The sun is still high in the sky and Maxwell said above ground in the area, or "biome", he was in, the worst he would have to face is a slime or the odd flying fish if it rained. He spots something in a small cave on the other side of a hill, it looks like a wooden chest but he cannot be sure. Feeling brave he gets out his shortsword and heads towards it, glancing back all the time to ensure the hut is still in sight.

Peering into the cave from the outside, Bert feels certain it is safe, he can see the wooden chest up ahead and he can see the back of the cave. There is nowhere in there for anything to lurk. He places a torch in the ground and walks in, pushing vines out of the way as he goes. He reaches the chest and lifts the lid, it opens easily but makes a loud creak that echoes around him. Inside are three identical red bottles, they are dusty and have labels that read "Lesser Healing Potion". Also in the chest is some rope and some bars of what looks like copper. He stashes them all in his pack and heads back out of the cave, feeling pleased with himself.

Before he has made it back through the cave entrance Bert knows something is wrong. The air smells rotten and he can hear a shuffling noise nearby. Suddenly what can only be a Zombie with greyish green skin, dressed in tattered filthy clothes, drops down in front of the entrance. It is followed by another, then two more. Bert grabs hold of his shortsword and takes a deep breath; Maxwell had told him Zombies never came out during the day. Never. What was going on?

The Zombies are still getting to their feet after falling from the roof of the cave, Bert makes use of this delay and runs out past them; knocking two back to the floor but barely missing the grabbing hands of another. He does not get far, however, before he comes face to face with four more Zombies closing in from the other direction. He turns to see the Zombies behind him are now mostly recovered and are gaining on him. Bert slashes at a few in front to try and make a space to run through, but his short sword does little damage. He is trapped. He really wishes Maxwell was here.

Chapter 7

Help from Above

A sudden blur of motion from above catches Bert's eye. Something purple streaks across the sky, it is moving unbelievably fast and as it passes over his head it drops something that lands inches from his feet, embedding itself point first into the grass. It takes him a second to recognise what he is looking at. A sword. A dark metal sword that looks like it has red twisting veins running around and through it.

Without thinking Bert grabs the hilt and pulls the strange sword free from the ground. It is noticeably longer than his current sword and also feels lighter and far stronger. Just holding it he knows it is a powerful weapon. He looks back up at the Zombies, which are now almost close enough to grab him, and he grins at them. This is more like it, he thinks, raising the sword.

Bert makes a long sideways slice at the four Zombies in front of him, the sword whistling through the air, knocking three of them to the floor and sending the fourth tumbling down a hill. He jumps forward and quickly finishes the three on the floor off before they get a chance to stand, a series of quick jabs turns them to piles of dust and empty clothes.

Noticing movement close behind, Bert spins round slicing the sword at the same time, it hits the Zombies that had been closing in behind him, sending them falling backwards. The light yet powerful sword quickly deals with them, leaving more piles of mouldy old clothes. Bert hears a groan and turns in time to see what appears to be an arm bone being swung at him like a club by the last remaining Zombie, it hits him in the side, his wood armour taking some of the damage, but he still feels the pain. He responds quickly, his sword blurs as he slices and strikes, turning his attacker to another pile of dust.

Bert looks at the ragged heaps of dirty and foul smelling old clothes, all that remains of the fallen Zombies. The "day Zombies". Scattered among them, glinting in the sun, are several coins. Bert reaches down and picks them up, careful not to touch the disgusting looking clothes. He also finds six wooden arrows and pops them in his pack as well.

As he walks back to his hut, Bert studies the sword, a strange looking combination of metal and red veins, sort of disgusting, he thinks, but he knows it saved his life today. He wonders who or what it was he saw, the purple blur that threw it to him. Had Maxwell returned or perhaps sent help? If so it could not have come at a better time.

He reaches the door to the hut and is so deep in thought he does not spot the thing hanging from it until he practically walks into it. He looks up to see a brown sack pinned to the door by a small four pointed silver throwing star, a shuriken, together with a note with four words on it.

"To keep you alive"

Chapter 8
Gift

Bert hopes to find Maxwell has returned as he opens the hut door, but it is empty inside, just as he left it. He puts the sack down on the work bench; it makes a solid metallic sounding thunk. He opens the string around the top and the sack falls open revealing what looks like a set of armour; deep purple in colour with an orange stripe. The helmet is a space age looking item with a pair of pointy orange wings sticking up on top and a dark glass visor.

Bert looks down at his uncomfy Wood armour and thinks it looks clumsy compared to the new armour. He checks the sack in case there is some sort of clue as to where or who it has come from, but there is nothing. He glances again at the note, shrugs, and decides to try the armour on.

Bert think perhaps most people would feel a bit silly wearing purple and orange armour, but as he looks down at himself all he can think is what a big improvement over his old armour it is. It feels comfy and light; he can tell it is strong. His side still aches from where the Zombie clubbed him with the arm bone, he feels certain he would have been protected from such a blow if he had been wearing this.

Bert heads outside the hut to get a better feel for the armour and to try and get to grips with the new sword. He does not put the helmet on, thinking it is not really necessary just for practicing. Not really knowing what to do he starts jumping and lunging with the sword, amazed at how quick and light it feels. He is mid leap, sword raised above his head, when a voice behind him speaks.

'Look at you! Someone's been busy.'

Surprised, he lands badly almost falling to the floor face first. He turns to see Maxwell, leaning on the door of the hut, grinning at him.

Chapter 9
The Guide Returns

Maxwell tells Bert he just got back after meeting with some of the NPCs and characters to whom he explained Bert's problem of being stuck outside of the tutorial in a dangerous world. He also spoke personally to Mike, one of the most respected characters, to ask for his advice.

'What do they all think then? What should I do?' Bert asks, keen to know how much longer he will be stuck in this world.

'Well, they're all surprised and worried about you, they agree they need to discuss it further. I'm to go back again tomorrow, Mike is arranging an emergency meeting to discuss what to do next. Listen, they're a smart bunch. Don't worry.'

'Did you tell them about all the slimes that attacked us?' Bert asks. Maxwell nods.

'Well you may want to mention this as well.' Maxwell frowns as Bert tells him about his fight with the "day Zombies", the purple something he saw flying through the sky, the sword and the armour. He hands Maxwell the note that came with the armour. The Guide's frown deepens.

'Zombies? During the day? It's just unheard of. And this sword, this the Blood Butcherer. It's a good sword, there are plenty more powerful weapons, but for the early game enemies this will make life much easier. And the armour, that's Meteor armour my friend. Have you tried it all on with the helmet?'

Bert shakes his head. Maxwell picks the helmet up and hands it to Bert who slips it over his head.

'Now try jumping.' Maxwell suggests. Bert looks at him confused.

'Go on!' Maxwell urges.

Bert jumps and as he does the suit comes to life, the surface shimmers as a shower of flames and sparks burst from the armour and trail behind him. Bert tries it out again. And again. Each movement he makes is trailed by the flames. Grinning he looks at Maxwell who is also smiling.

'That,' Bert says 'is so cool! Now I really am Blazing Bert.'

Maxwell decides he will get to the meeting tomorrow earlier than planned so he can tell Mike about the latest developments.

'Can't they come here to have the meeting?' Bert asks.

'No way I'm afraid. Nobody can get in or out of this world it seems, nobody apart from me. They think that I'm only here because each new world gets assigned a Guide and somehow I'm the Guide for this place. You arriving here must have somehow caused me to come here. Oh, before I forget, Mike gave me this to give to you.' Maxwell hands over a rolled up piece of paper which Bert opens reveal a neatly written note.

"Blazing Bert. Welcome to Terraria, sorry it has not been a great start for you. We promise we will all do everything we can to rescue you and get you safely to the tutorial. Maxwell will look out for you, he is a good Guide and a good friend to have. Whatever you do, stay safe. We all hope to meet you really soon.
Your friend,
Mike"

Chapter 10

Gone

That night in his dreams Bert is wandering around maze like underground tunnels, being chased by Zombies. He is heading towards a red light and when he finally gets to it, he realises it is a red heart. Shocked, he steps back and starts to fall. Suddenly he is awake.

He looks around the hut and for a moment cannot figure out what is wrong. Then it occurs to him. Maxwell is nowhere to be seen. On the work bench, on the back of the note from Mike, Maxwell has left a message in large scruffy handwriting.

"Morning sleeping beauty! Didn't want to wake you. Gone to the cave where the day Zombies attacked you to look for clues. Back soon. M"

For some reason Bert has a nervous feeling in the pit of his stomach, something feels wrong. He grabs his armour and Blood Butcherer sword and heads outside.

Bert retraces his steps back towards the cave. Reaching the hill from where he first spotted the chest, he can see no sign of the Guide. There does, however, appear to be something green glowing from inside the cave. The nervous feeling inside increases as he pulls the Meteor helmet from his pack and slides it over his head. Immediately his suit comes to life, blazing and sparkling. But he does not even notice as he runs towards the glowing light, sword raised.

The green glow seems to be coming from something splattered on the cave walls, he knows it was definitely not there yesterday. He quickly checks around for enemies before heading inside the cave, he does not want to get trapped again like yesterday. It seems safe, he thinks he spots a slime way off in the distance but not near enough to worry about yet. As he walks into the cave he can see the green goo is not randomly splattered on the wall, it is in fact writing. A message. To him.

"B.B. I have the Guide. If you want to see him again head to the red hills of the Crimson tomorrow at nightfall. Follow my Eye and my Brain. I will be waiting for you. Cthulhu"

Chapter 11

Slimy

Bert stumbles out of the cave. Somebody has taken Maxwell, but what did it mean, follow my Eye and my Brain? And who is Cthulhu? What is the Crimson? He feels dizzy trying to understand it all. The slime he spotted earlier in the distance is still slowly heading towards him, but he does not pay it any attention. One slime he can deal with, he has much bigger problems to worry about.

As he walks past the piles of clothes left over from the Zombie fight yesterday, Bert spots something poking out of the ground. It is a wooden arrow, one of Maxwell's arrows. So he must have put up a fight with who or whatever took him. He reaches down to pull the arrow out the ground and spots something next to it. It looks like a small red light with a wire trailing out of it. As he examines it he can see it is cracked and slightly crushed, as if someone or something has trodden on it.

While reaching round to put the light into his pack, Bert spots movement, it is the same slime still approaching, but as he looks harder he can see something gleaming on the top of its head, something golden, he also realises the slime itself is a lot bigger than the other slimes he has seen. It was just so far away he had not realised quite how big until now.

The giant slime approaches, coming towards him in great long leaps, covering the distance between them quickly. It is nearly three times his own size and he can now see the gold on its head is actually a crown. Bert does not want to go backwards towards the cave, he would only be trapped there. Plus he does not want to move further away from his hut, he realises he has no choice; he has to face the crown wearing giant slime.

Bert takes a deep breath, the slime has stopped in front of him out of reach of his sword. It makes a gloopy liquid noise and wobbles like an oversized jelly. It seems to be regarding him. Not knowing what else to do, Bert raises his sword ready to strike when, as if by some unspoken order, several smaller slimes of varying colours all leap out from hiding behind the larger one, the same trick they played on him and Maxwell yesterday, hiding behind each other, and he fell for it again. The smaller slimes start throwing themselves in his direction.

Bert knows he is vastly outnumbered, he fights desperately, slashing and stabbing whenever one of them gets too close. Some of them seem tougher than others, especially the spiked ones and the ones that appear to be made of lava. They are slowly pushing Bert back towards the cave, he knows in there he will be trapped with no way of escape. All the while he can see the massive leader looming over them all, watching the fight but not yet joining in.

Bert hears a noise coming from inside the cave behind him. A whirring noise and what sounds like rocks clattering, but he cannot turn to look or the slimes will overpower him. He takes another step back, when his foot bashes into a rock and he begins to trip and fall backwards. Not good, he thinks as the mass of slimes hurtle towards him, not good at all.

Chapter 12

Help

It feels like everything is moving in slow motion as Bert loses his balance and falls backwards to the ground. In this moment he notices several things happening. The slimes are nearly on him, they know they have won as they leap at him. Behind them he can see the giant leader begin to take a massive bounding jump in his direction, as if it senses he is beaten and wants to finish him off. He can also hear a strange whooshing noise coming from behind him. Suddenly he is bathed in a bright pink light. Bert hits the floor and where he was standing just moments before is what looks like a sword made of pink light flying through the air straight into the pack of slimes. The light sword strikes several of the slime and they either burst apart defeated or are knocked away by the force.

Bert hears a voice from the cave behind him, a girl's voice, 'Hey, you on the floor. Unless you wanna become a snack for the King Slime I suggest you get up and get into this cave.'

Scrambling to his feet, Bert turns to see the cave is filled with a bright pink light, the light source is coming from the back, low to the floor. It appears to be a small glowing creature with white fluttering wings. He can see it is directly in front of a hole in the wall at the back of the cave.

The voice calls again, coming from the direction of the hole. 'Come on, what are you waiting for? Get into the tunnel and make it snappy.'

Bert glances around to see the King Slime leap closer. Wasting no more time he darts towards the back of the cave, jumping to the floor as he reaches the far end. He climbs head first into the small opening, the winged light disappears further down the tunnel ahead of him as he makes his way inside crawling on his hands and knees as quickly as he can. He has only made it a short way when something goes flying past his head back in the direction of the cave, barely missing him. Bert looks over his shoulder to see the object land on the cave floor, it is a stick of dynamite, a stick of dynamite with a lit fuse.

Bert yells and scrambles frantically further down the tunnel, chasing after the winged light. All of a sudden the floor of the tunnel is no longer beneath him and he is falling. He drops a short distance then lands in a heap.

Looking up from the ground, Bert sees the face of a girl looking back at him, the winged light is fluttering over her shoulder and she is grinning widely, hands pressed over her ears.

'Cover your ears!' the girl shouts and Bert just manages to get his hands to his own ears when an enormous BOOM fills the world.

Chapter 13
Ruby

The cave shakes and shudders from the huge explosion made by the dynamite. Rocks, stones and a shower of dust fall around Bert where he lays on the floor, hands still pressed to his ears. Eventually, when all seems quiet again, he gets up and dusts himself off. He aches in several places and his ears are ringing, but apart from that he seems to be undamaged. The armour has done its job and has protected him from any serious harm.

Bert appears to be in an underground cave, he looks up to the hole he had crawled through only moments ago, it is now blocked with rocks and rubble following the explosion. The mysterious dynamite throwing girl is currently rummaging through her pack tutting to herself. She is wearing pinkish armour, including a helmet topped with two dangerous looking metal spikes. Finally she seems to find what she is looking for.

'Aha, here we go.' she hands Bert a torch which emits a white glow. 'That should do you until you get yourself a light pet.'

'Light pet?' Bert asks, confused. She points to the white winged, glowing light fluttering next to her.

'Oh, I see,' says Bert, 'well thanks for the torch. And for saving me back there. I'm Bert by the way.'

'I know.' she says. 'Come on, let's get out of here.' she walks off quickly, her winged light pet fluttering next to her, illuminating the way.

'Wait!' Bert calls, 'Who are you? Where are we going? What's going on?'

'Questions questions, so many questions.' she replies with a sigh, 'Let's keep moving, I'll fill you in as best I can on the way.'

'My name is Ruby.' she says, she has a high girlish voice and talks quickly, 'I'm the one who's been keeping you alive. I gave you the sword and the armour and I just saved you from King Slime and his gooey buddies.'

'Wow OK. Well thanks again then I guess. How did you save me by the way? What was that pink sword thing that hit the pack of slimes back there?'

Ruby turns round and smiles, 'That would be my sword, True Excalibur.' she pulls out a long impressive looking sword with a huge red jewel in its hilt. Bert is about to point out that was not the pink sword he saw earlier, when Ruby swings the weapon and firing out of it comes a pink version of itself made of light, which shoots down a tunnel. It hits something, there is a high pitch squeak and what appears to be a bat drops to the floor.

'Wow!' is all Bert manages to say.

'I know.' agrees Ruby.

'Ok, so what about the tunnel we just came from at the back of the cave? I know that was not there yesterday.' Bert points out, trying to make sense of one thing at a time.

'I just mined it,' Ruby replies, 'I've got a pretty good drill, only took a couple of minutes. You looked trapped by those slime, seemed the best way to get you out and do some damage to that ugly slime boss at the same time.'

They walk through various caves and tunnels, but Ruby seems to know where she is going so Bert follows without question.

'So you were the purple streak I saw yesterday in the sky that threw me the sword? Why didn't you come and help me fight those Zombies?' Bert asks.

Ruby stops and turns to look at him, a puzzled look on her face.

'I did help, I gave you the sword didn't I?' she then seems to get cross and pokes him in the chest, 'Listen Blazing Barney, if you want to survive out here, you have to learn to fight for yourself, you seem to be OK with a sword, you just need to fall over a bit less. But here's a lesson I'll give you for free. Nobody tells me what to do. Now do you want my help or not?'

She does not wait for an answer but turns and walks off. Bert quickly follows keeping quiet, deciding he will make an effort to stay on Ruby's good side.

Chapter 14
Tunnels and Traps

Bert and Ruby make their way through various twisting tunnels and underground caves, they wade through shallow water and climb wooden platforms that seem to have been constructed to make moving to higher or lower areas easier.

The path Ruby takes always seems to be dotted with lit torches. Occasionally they meet an enemy, mostly slimes, Ruby deals with those in her path with a flick of her True Excalibur sword, barely seeming to pay them any attention. Bert takes care of a few that come close to him, he wants to prove he is not relying on Ruby to fight for him. He still has so many questions to ask, but after making her angry earlier he thinks he will wait for her to break the silence.

'See that?' she says after what must have been half an hour of travelling without speaking. She points with her sword, Bert can only see a greyish block in front.

'What is it?' he asks, squinting to make out what she is talking about.

'Watch.' she says, she presses the floor in front of her with her sword, and then from the grey block a dart shoots out and smashes into her sword. Ruby picks up the dart and shows it to Bert.

'Poison dart trap. Activated by this pressure plate on the floor. You gotta watch for those. There are plenty of them hidden below the surface, but never normally this high up. We're in the Underground, if we head further down eventually we'll be in the Caverns, that's where you'd normally find these. Someone has been here since I mined it out and they've set this trap up just for us, we had better watch our step, literally.'

They make their way carefully around the trap and Bert asks, 'So you put all these torches and platforms here?'

'Yup. Glad I did, turned out to be a good escape route to get you out of that cave.'

'So where are we going?' Bert asks, pleased Ruby is talking again.

'I've got a few bases setup around this world, I need to get to one to get some supplies ready for tomorrow.'

'Tomorrow?' Bert questions.

'Yeah, tomorrow night. You read the writing on the cave right? We've got a Guide to save.'

Bert feels so relieved to hear her say that. The thought of rescuing Maxwell by himself, meeting some sort of brain and eye, is not a pleasant one. With Ruby helping he feels sure they can get him back.

Chapter 15

Dizzy Heights

Feeling much happier knowing he has Ruby on his side, Bert starts asking questions again, too many questions. Ruby eventually stops him.

'Listen, I get it. You're all full of questions, you're bursting with them. Do me a favour and let's get somewhere safe so we can have a sit down, a nice little chat, and I'll answer what I can. But for now let me concentrate, OK?'

Bert takes a breath, he was about to ask another question, but he holds it in and simply nods. Ruby nods back, pleased with this response.

'Now then, follow me and stay close and I will get us out of here in no time flat.'

They keep travelling, always heading up. They have to avoid several more dart traps along the way. After a while Bert sees light coming from above, he clambers up a wooden platform and has to squint as he finds himself looking down a tunnel that comes out above ground, daylight streaming in.

'Wait there.' Ruby calls, dashing off ahead, moving so fast she seems to blur. She comes back a short while later, 'It's clear, no enemies around at the moment. Let's go, but stay really close.'

Bert emerges from the cave to find himself in a cold white landscape. Snow-capped mountains, leafless trees with white topped branches and a layer of crunchy snow covering the ground in all directions. He looks around amazed at how different it looks from the land where he built his hut. Ruby is already walking off, but stops when she sees Bert standing there staring at his surroundings.

'Welcome to the Snow biome Barney.' she says.

They crunch off through the snow, Bert trusts Ruby knows where she is going and once again follows without question. They meet few enemies on the way, the ones they do meet are not powerful and are taken care of quickly. Ruby is quiet and watchful all the time.

After climbing a particularly steep hill above a frozen pool of water, rather abruptly, the scenery changes. One moment they are walking on a carpet of snow and the next, the land is all green grass and leafy trees.

They continue on for a while until they find themselves at a tree so tall Bert cannot see the top. There are several chunks cut out the side of the wide trunk which Ruby uses as hand and foot holds, climbing with apparent ease. Bert follows less easily and tries not to look down as they get higher and higher. Eventually they find themselves standing on the top branches, Bert can see all around. In one direction he can see the green land they are currently in, turning to the snowy land they came though and after that dark red hills and trees. In the other direction he can see more green hills and eventually what looks like yellow sand and further away still the endless sparkling blue of what can only be the ocean.

Bert is about to comment on the view to Ruby, but when he turns he finds she is no longer standing next to him. He panics, thinking she must have fallen, when a voice above calls, 'Hey, you coming or what?'

He looks up to see Ruby hanging from a rope that seems to disappear up into the clouds.

Chapter 16

Head in the Clouds

Bert dares a quick look down, he thought he was high up when he was on top of the tree, but now he is hanging from a rope and the tree is a distant green dot below him. He swallows and looks upwards instead. Ruby is far ahead of him and he still cannot see where the rope ends, it simply goes up and up through the clouds high above.

Ruby had thrown him down a device which attached onto the rope and when he put his weight on it, it started pulling him upwards. She told him if he turned it round the other way it would lower him downwards safely. He was relieved as he knew there was no way he would be able to climb that high with his bare hands.

Bert watches as Ruby disappears through a gap in the cloud above and he soon finds himself heading through it. He comes out the top of the cloud and his rope device stops. The rope has come to an end, tied up around a rock. The rock is on a patch of grassy ground on top of the cloud. Grass on top of a cloud! Bert shakes his head in amazement.

'Come on then.' Ruby calls, she is a short distance from the hole, hands on her hips, scanning the surrounding area with an impatient expression on her face.

Bert pulls himself up and looks around what would appear to be an island on a cloud. The land on top of the cloud island is flat. There are a few trees and what looks like a yellow and blue bricked house in one direction. In the other direction he can see grass, then cloud and then endless sky. Bert walks to where the grassy ground becomes cloud, Ruby walks over beside him.

'You want to see something really cool?'

Bert looks at Ruby warily but nods. Without warning she shoves him forward. His arms windmill around, trying to catch his balance before he falls through the cloud, but it is too late and he steps over the edge. He expects to fall but instead his feet step onto solid ground, he is standing on cloud.

Bert looks around at Ruby who is smiling wickedly, 'That was not funny.' he says, catching his breath.

'I totally disagree.' Ruby says, then she does an impression of him with his arms spinning around trying to balance. The look on her face as she mimics him is so funny that despite himself Bert laughs too and then they are both laughing hysterically, unable to stop.

Something blue whooshes through the air and embeds itself into the surface of the cloud inches from Bert's feet. It appears to be a feather, but razor sharp. The laughter is instantly gone from Ruby's face, she has her sword in hand and is slicing it through the air in a blur of movement, pink light swords shooting towards the source of the feather. Bert can see something flying towards them, it is a human-ish figure but with blue feathered wings and something definitely not quite human about its face, especially the eyes. It flings more of the feathers in their direction.

'Harpies,' Ruby shouts, 'get to the house, I'll deal with them.'

Chapter 17
Feathered Pests

Bert starts to run, he keeps looking back over his shoulder and can see Ruby expertly ducking and dodging feathers and swooping Harpies. The cloud lights up pink she fires off more swords from her True Excalibur. He runs in the direction of the house as instructed and shouts.

'Come on, let's get inside.'

'Be there in a sec. Let me just get rid of these feathered pests.'

Bert jumps over the hole they just climbed through. Feathers hit the floor around him not far from where his feet had been moments before. A couple strike his armour but he keeps moving, ignoring the pain.

Bert reaches the door of the house and turns to see Ruby still fighting furiously. A Harpy zooms overhead, heading for her. He swipes at it with his sword but misses. He then watches as Ruby jumps impossibly high and strikes down two surprised Harpies circling above her head. She lands and immediately fires off a pink sword which strikes the one that just passed over Bert, it comes crashing to the ground.

The sky finally seems clear of enemies. Bert watches as Ruby bends to pick something up from the ground near a fallen Harpy. At that moment he spots what looks like a dark cloud behind her heading straight at her, moving fast. He points and shouts as the cloud gets closer, Ruby turns and raises her sword just as the shape comes crashing into her. The force of it knocks her off her feet and sends her sword flying from her hand and tumbling off the edge of the Floating Island.

The dark shape that struck Ruby is now past her and heading straight towards Bert instead. He stands outside the door to the sky house and watches in horror. It seems to be a huge mass of flying eyeballs, each at least the size of a football, all crowded together and moving as one, all staring at him.

Ruby shouts at the top of her voice, 'Get inside. NOW!' bringing Bert to his senses. He throws open the door and scrambles inside. He closes the door just in time, there are several loud thumps as the eyes crash into it. After a few moments Bert opens the door a crack and peers out, he can see the eyes have re-grouped and are heading back towards Ruby for a second attack. She is facing them head on, Bert thinks any normal person in her position would look scared, but the look on her face is far from scared, she looks angry.

He watches as Ruby points at the eyeballs and yells, 'You made me drop my sword. I like that sword. It goes with my outfit.' she then reaches in her pack and pulls out a large spiked black and white ball on the end of a chain. 'This does not go with my outfit,' she says pointing at the weapon, 'so I'm gonna make this real quick.'

She leaps into the air and the spiked ball darts away from her as she swings it into the pack of eyeballs. They are scattered by the force of her attack, some falling to the ground defeated, others flying off dazed. Several more swings of the weapon and she has taken care of every single one of the eyes.

Ruby spots Bert and waves cheerily at him calling out, 'You'd better get inside, I've just gotta go and get my sword. Be back in a tick.' before Bert has time react, Ruby leaps of the edge of the cloud and disappears into the blue sky below.

Chapter 18

Courage

Bert runs out of the house heading to the edge of the cloud. He peers over the dizzying drop, but cannot see anything apart from the distant ground below. Ruby just jumped, he cannot understand why, what was she thinking?

Something strikes the armour on Bert's back and he looks over his shoulder to see a Harpy flying straight at him, firing sharp blue feathers in his direction. He holds his sword ready but does not turn to face it, not yet. He waits until it is really close and then spins and slices at it. The Harpy shrieks and flies off, it throws a couple of feathers but he is ready and dodges them easily. The Harpy circles back around and Bert makes a decision, he is not going to run from it, he is going to face it head on.

Bert starts running in the direction of the Harpy. It flies straight towards him, firing more feathers but Bert dodges them and keeps running. As he gets to the rock with the rope tied to it, he bounds up on to it and uses it as a step to jump as high in the air as he can, sword raised over his head. Suddenly he is eye level with the Harpy which is looking back at him, a surprised expression on its face. In that moment the enemy hesitates and Bert brings his raised sword down on it. The Harpy falls to the ground in a feathered heap. Bert lands near it and lets out a whoosh of breath. He cannot believe he just did that.

He hears someone clapping behind him and turns to see Ruby, hovering above the ground, wearing a pair of huge purpley pink butterfly wings which are flapping lazily. In her hand is her True Excalibur sword.

'Not a bad job with that Harpy Blazing Barney, not bad at all. But didn't I tell you to wait in the house?'

'You did,' Bert replies, ignoring the fact she called him Barney again, 'but you also told me I have to learn to fight for myself, I thought I'd better take your advice.'

She grins widely at him, 'Good point, I do give good advice.'

'Got your sword back then?' Bert asks.

'Yup.'

'What was it you stopped to pick up before those eyeball things knocked into you?'

'Those were demon eyes, they never travel in groups like that though. That was really weird. The thing I picked up was a Giant Harpy Feather, it's an ingredient you can use to craft wings, always worth having wings. Just in case.'

Bert nods looking at hers.

'Why didn't you just fly up here to start with? Why climb the rope?' he asks.

'Question time again is it?' she responds rolling her eyes. 'Well I had to show you how to get up here. Anyway, you've gotta learn how to do things round here the hard way as well as the easy way. Plus I wouldn't want you thinking I like to show off. Actually forget that, I love to show off. Now, shall we head inside? We've got plans to make and a Guide to find.'

Chapter 19

Up and Away

The sky house is small, even compared to Bert's hut. Most of the floor is taken up by a chair, table and a blue chest with a yellow pattern on the front.

'Take a look in the chest.' Ruby suggests. She is busy scanning the floor, looking for something.

Bert opens the chest, inside are a few more of the red lesser healing potions, a small pile of copper coins and a gold horseshoe. 'What's this?' he asks, holding up the horseshoe.

Ruby looks up and then back down to continue her search. 'That's a Lucky Horseshoe, pretty good find. Hang on to it, it has powers that will reduce damage if you fall a long way.'

'Cool,' says Bert, feeling pleased but also hoping he never has need of it. 'So what are you looking for?'

'Aha! This.' she says, kicking a bit of floor that, to Bert, looks the same as the rest of the floor. She reaches into her pack and produces a cone shaped drill and proceeds to start noisily churning up the stone floor of the house with it. Bert watches, assuming whatever Ruby is doing will make sense in a minute. He is right. Hidden just under the floor is a chest, she opens it and starts rummaging around inside, talking to herself as she does.

'Ah, I could do with one of these. Oh sweet, I forgot I had this. So that's where I left this.'

Eventually she comes away with an armful of things that she drops onto the floor. From the pile she picks up a pair of yellow boots with white wings on the sides and throws them in Bert's direction without looking up.

'Here, put these on then go outside and try jumping and running.' she instructs.

'What are they?' Bert asks.

'Lightning Boots!' Ruby replies, now looking up, a wide smile spread across her face. Bert slips the boots on and walks to the door.

'If you see any bad guys,' Ruby calls, 'just come back in or give me a shout, OK?'

Walking outside in the Lightning Boots, Bert can feel the difference instantly, he feels quick and light on his feet. He dashes around for a bit, marvelling at how fast it feels. He then jumps and to his utter surprise the boots make a whooshing noise and he finds his jump goes up and up. He is flying.

Bert looks down at his feet; the boots are letting out white puffs of vapour as he shoots upwards. He whoops happily, he cannot believe he is actually flying. However, quite suddenly, the boots stop and he is no longer flying, he is falling. Bert lands on the roof of the house, just managing to stay on his feet. He prepares himself to feel some pain in his legs from the heavy fall, but it never comes. He remembers the Lucky Horseshoe and realises it must have prevented some of the damage; suddenly he is very thankful for finding it.

Bert tries flying several more times, understanding that for each jump the boots only have so much power. He realises the trick is to save a bit of it to use just before landing to prevent falling too hard. Once he has figured this out the fun really starts. This is amazing, Bert thinks, laughing out loud.

Chapter 20

Q & A

Bert walks back into the sky house to find Ruby transformed, from the girl in the pink armour with butterfly wings, she is now wearing a silvery armour tinged with blue. There are large spikes sticking out of the back and a spiked matching helmet is currently sat on the table. Without her helmet Bert sees she has dark blue hair worn up in a ponytail. She has a long trident in one hand and a sword in the other and keeps looking from one to the other, both appear to be made of the same metal as her armour.

'What do you think Barney, the trident or the sword? The trident is weaker but has a good reach, whereas the sword is stronger but means getting in closer to fight. But most importantly, which one looks better? Does the trident make me look short?'

'It's Bert, not Barney, and no, if anything the trident makes you look more dangerous than the sword. All those sharp points together with that spiked armour.'

She looks at the trident and nods approvingly. 'Trident it is then.'

'So that was your chest you dug up I'm guessing?'

'Yeah,' she agrees, putting the sword away, 'I tend to hide my stuff in chests in the worlds I visit, just in case.'

'So you're a character like me then, not an NPC?' She nods.

'I'm a character, but I'm stuck here just like you. I visited a long time ago when I was newly created. I came back a few days ago looking for one of my old chests but spotted some weird behaviour from the enemies in the world. I decided to stay to investigate, but when I went to leave I realised I couldn't. Someone has been messing with this world and they've managed to lock it. Nobody, character or NPC can get in or out of here. Nobody that is, apart from your Guide friend.'

'So are the problems with this world, the large groups of slimes, the "day Zombies", the writing in the cave and the big pack of demon eyes, are they all part of the same problem, the problem that means we can't leave this world?' Bert asks.

'Hey, you are catching on fast. I think they must be, whoever has locked this world has also done something to the enemies to make them act strange.' Ruby replies.

'And that same person, or thing, now has Maxwell?'

'Looks like.'

'And once we've dealt with them I am free to leave this world?'

'Yup.'

'Then let's find this Cthulhu and rescue Maxwell.'

Ruby grins, 'I like the sound of that.'

Chapter 21
Upgrades

Bert wakes the next morning with a groan, he feels achy from yesterday's adventures and from another uncomfortable night's sleep. It had been a restless night as he had been worrying about, well, everything.

Last night Ruby had explained that the eye and brain which the note on the cave wall mentions, are probably the Eye and Brain of Cthulhu, two early game bosses. They are a giant eyeball and a giant brain, yuck, Bert thinks. She also told him Cthulhu is not a boss or a character in the game, so whoever signed the note must be just using the name.

Stretching to try and ease some of his aches, Bert looks round to see Ruby coming into the hut from outside, the long and deadly looking silver-blue trident in hand. She is plucking what looks like a blue Harpy feather from the middle prong of the fork ended spear.

'Good morning sunshine!' she says cheerily after glancing at Bert's sleepy and, no doubt, worried looking face.

'Been busy?' Bert asks, watching the feather drift to the floor.

Ruby shrugs. 'No more than usual. Listen, I've been thinking, you could do with some upgrades. We don't know what we'll be facing today. Normally I don't give my stuff away, but this is only your third day in the game and what's happening round here is not normal.'

Ruby reaches into her pack and produces a long dark purple sword, she clunks it down on the table. 'This is Night's Edge, it's pretty tough, tougher than the Blood Butcherer you've been using.'

Rummaging some more, she pulls out several red bottles all labelled "Healing Potion" and also produces some plates of what looks like cooked fish. Finally she places five red sparkling crystal hearts gently on the table.

'Eat a Cooked Fish now and save the rest for later, you'll feel better all over for a while. If you get hurt, drink a red potion to heal some of the damage.

The hearts are Life Crystals, break them open in your hands now and your overall health will be increased.'

'Thanks, this is great. You always seem to be keeping me safe, I do appreciate it.'

Ruby shrugs, looking a little embarrassed, 'Hey whatever. Don't mention it. Just look after my sword OK?'

Bert nods, picking up Night's Edge and moving it from side to side. To his surprise, as it moves dark purple sparks of light trail behind it. 'Cool!' he says to himself, feeling his worries lessen at the sight of the powerful sword.

'So where and what is this Crimson we're heading for then?' Bert asks, still watching the sword make trailing purple patterns in the air as he moves it. Ruby explains that each new world created has infected areas, or biomes, full of tougher baddies. A world will either have purple biomes called the Corruption or it will have red biomes called the Crimson. For this world it is Crimson and that is where they have to go.

Chapter 22

Travelling in Style

Within seconds of leaving the house Bert is soaked through, the skies are dark and it is raining heavily. They lower themselves back down the long rope from the cloud island. Bert tries hard not to look down at the dizzying drop and Ruby busies herself flinging shurikens at some Flying Fish who look like they might try and attack.

They cross the Snow biome they travelled through the previous day and pass the entrance to the cave they had emerged from after the King Slime attack. Bert enjoys the quick pace the Lightning Boots give him and the ability to fly is not only hugely fun, but also means he can get over some of the harder to climb areas with ease. Ruby chooses to climb and jump, she still makes it look easy.

They reach a very tall and sheer cliff; Bert notices it seems to turn from a frosty white at the bottom to a dark red at the top. The Crimson.

Standing at the bottom of the cliff, looking over to Ruby, Bert asks, 'Are you going to put your Butterfly Wings on to get up there then?'

Ruby looks at him as if he just said something very rude. 'Purple Butterfly Wings with Titanium armour. That would not go. I would look ridiculous!'

'Err, right. So how are you going to get up there?'

Ruby glances upwards to the top of the cliff, she does not seem particularly bothered by the height of it. 'Oh I'll figure something out, go on then Barney, see you in the Crimson.'

'It's Bert, you know it is.'

Ruby just smiles in response. Bert leaps into the air; the cliff is tall enough that he has to land half way up on a jutting out rock. He thinks he hears something behind him but does not have time to turn and look. He takes another leap and lands at the top. To his surprise Ruby is already there.

'Took your time, *Bert*.' she says, emphasising his name. She is standing on a blue board that is floating a foot off the ground; a bright blue light shining underneath it. Ruby grins at the look on his face.

'Wow, that's a cool…' he does not know what the thing she is standing on is called.

'Oh, my Hoverboard, yeah it's pretty awesome.' she grins and whooshes off. Bert is beginning to realise that Ruby always seems to have another trick up her sleeve.

Chapter 23

Crimson

The Crimson, Bert discovers, is a gloomy place. It is covered in dark red grass and the trees have dark trunks with blood red coloured leaves drooping from them. Even the pools of water appear to be red. Also there are noticeably more caves and dangerous drops.

The first Crimson enemy Bert encounters looks like a person from a distance, but as it gets closer he realises it is covered in brown dirty looking fur and has a large, long mouth which remains hanging open, displaying a set of dangerous looking fangs. Ruby tells him it is called a Face Monster, they defeat it but before long they are facing another, and then another. The Face Monsters are then joined by large flying bugs, Crimera, Ruby informs him. Dark red in colour with wicked looking pincers, they circle Bert and Ruby and then without warning fly in quickly to attack. Ruby's trident darts and flashes through the air sending enemies flying. Bert's Night's Edge sword blazes purple striking anything that comes close. The enemies keep on coming and they make slow progress over the Crimson landscape.

Eventually they get to a hut, they run inside to take shelter from the constant attack of the enemies.

'Phew, they are coming thick and fast today.' Ruby says, although she does not seem overly concerned or out of breath. Bert, on the other hand feels worn out.

Ruby suggests he should have another cooked fish, and drink a healing potion to heal some of the damage he had received fighting the swarming enemies.

Before long Bert is feeling much better. He looks over to Ruby who has an ear pressed to the door. 'Hear that?' she asks in a whisper.

Bert, mouth still full of cooked fish, shakes his head, he cannot hear anything.

'Exactly, it's quiet, no moaning, growling, hissing or howling. It's weird, we're in the Crimson, normally there's always a baddy on the prowl. Silence is not normal.'

She opens the door a crack and peers out, then opens it wider. Eventually, after looking around, she tells Bert to wait there and disappears outside, closing the door behind her.

Bert does not have to wait long before Ruby pokes her spiky helmeted head back through the door, a confused look on her face.

'What's happening then?' Bert asks, impatient to know.

'Um, I don't really know.'

'Well, is it safe?'

'Yeah, I mean no, I mean, well, you'd better come out here and take a look.'

Bert follows Ruby outside, there are no enemies immediately attacking them, he takes this as a good sign. Ruby points ahead into the distance, all Bert can see is trees and the dark silhouettes of some tall hills or mountains. He is looking to the sky when he notices one of the hills is moving. He looks closer and realises the dark shapes are not hills, but are the silhouettes of two very large creatures of some sort, and they are just floating there. As they walk closer Bert realises what he is looking at is a large and very gross eyeball and next to it an equally large and equally gross giant brain.

Chapter 24

Eye and Brain

Bert gulps. When Ruby described the Eye and Brain of Cthulhu he had not realised how big they would be. They are bigger than the hut he has just left. Is he seriously expected to fight these things?

'So what exactly do we do now?' Bert asks Ruby, pleased his voice is not shaking.

'Not sure.' Ruby replies, 'You see, they're bosses. Bosses normally don't just float there ignoring you, they zoom at you, all teeth and tentacles. And they don't naturally stay near each other like that. It's creepy.'

Bert thinks there is a lot creepy about this situation.

'Well, the note said to follow the eye and the brain, maybe we should go closer and see what they do.' Bert suggests, even though getting closer to them is the last thing he wants to do, but he thinks of Maxwell and walks towards them. Ruby is by his side with her trident raised. When they get close enough to be in the shadow of the bosses, the two monsters slowly turn away from them and float off heading further into the Crimson. Bert looks at Ruby, she seems puzzled but shrugs and follows. As they walk Ruby keeps glancing around, she seems to sense a trap and Bert knows how she feels.

'I think the other enemies are staying away from these two uglies. It's night now and this place would normally be overrun, but look around, not a Face Monster in sight. I don't think we're the only ones who can sense something strange is happening here.' Ruby says.

Eventually they reach a large cave opening. The bosses wait for Bert and Ruby to catch up and then start heading into the cave. Bert is just about to follow when something catches his eye, over the other side of the cave behind some rocks, he is sure he sees a figure moving. He stops to look and Ruby walks into the back of him.

'Hey, what is it?' She asks, looking to where Bert is staring.

'Thought I saw someone.'

'I can't see anything,' she says, 'come on, let's get this over with.'

At that moment something red streaks through the sky and Bert does not even have time to cry out or warn Ruby when it lands behind her, only just missing her. Ruby twists and Bert can see an arrow with a red blinking light on the end sticking out of her pack. Neither of them have any time to do anything about this as arrows start raining down on them, forcing Bert into the cave and Ruby to hide behind a rock outside. Bert notices movement over his shoulder and he turns just in time to see the giant Brain of Cthulhu fade and disappear.

Bert shouts to Ruby, 'Err, I know this is probably not the best time, but the brain just vanished. It disappeared in front of my eyes.'

'It teleported,' she yells back, 'they do that. Just watch out for where it…"'

She does not have time to finish as the gap between them is suddenly filled with the shape of the enormous brain. It floats there for a long moment, then with a roar it flies towards Ruby, the sky around it filling with large beach ball sized eyeballs all circling it protectively.

Bert hears Ruby shout, 'Get into the cave. RUN!'

Chapter 25

A Crazy Idea

Bert has not been around long, three days to be precise. He does not yet know what sort of a person he is. Is he funny, kind, forgetful, a bit weird? He simply does not know. But in that moment when Ruby is attacked by the Brain of Cthulhu and all its minions, he discovers he knows one thing about himself. He is not going to be the type of person to leave a friend in trouble. Even if she has just told him to.

Bert tries to spot Ruby to see if she is safe, but the brain is so big his view is blocked. Then suddenly in a burst of blue light there she is, flying on her Hoverboard, her trident is nowhere to be seen, instead she seems to be drawing back a light blue, icy looking bow. Even during all the chaos, Bert marvels at the fact she is using a bow which matches her armour and Hoverboard.

The Brain chases Ruby as she zooms off, the beach ball sized eyeballs still surrounding it; she seems to be targeting them rather than the brain. What is it with this place and eyeballs, Bert thinks, it's just plain weird. The thought gives Bert an idea. A crazy idea. An idea so crazy he wonders if he is really thinking it. He looks into the cave to where the Eye of Cthulhu is still waiting, patiently bobbing in the air.

Bert starts shouting at the eye 'Hey you, ugly big eyeball, yeah you. Look at me, over here. Come and fight me blinky. Come on. Come and get me.' the eye is unaware of his abuse, it still just seems to be waiting for him to follow it. Frustrated Bert picks up a stone and throws it at the eye, it bounces uselessly off surface of the eye back into the cave wall and hits something. Bert glances over to where the stone landed and spots, jutting out from behind a rock, a long thin piece of wood. He walks over and finds it is actually a bow. He picks it up and cannot help but notice it looks a lot like the bow Maxwell used when they first met.

Bert checks around but cannot find any arrows. That would be too convenient. He then remembers the arrows he picked up after his fight with the Zombies. He reaches into his pack and pulls out six wooden arrows. He loads one into the bow and fires, he hits the eye but it gives no reaction, he fires three more but nothing seems to be getting the eyes attention. Not knowing what else to do Bert jumps, his boots propel him up towards the roof of the cave and above the giant eyeball. Whilst in the air he shoots an arrow towards the top of the eye, the arrow hits and he can see next to where it has struck is a small flashing red light, like the one he found on the floor after Maxwell was first taken. Like the one in the arrow that was just shot at Ruby. He suddenly knows what he needs to do.

Bert takes a deep breath and jumps again. In the air he aims for the small light and tries to keep the bow steady, it is his last arrow, he thinks of his new friends Maxwell and Ruby, both in need of help. He cannot let them down. Slowly he releases the arrow and watches it sail at the giant eye, to his amazement it hits the blinking red light which fizzes and stops flashing. The effect on the Eye of Cthulhu is instant, it swivels to look directly at Bert, emits a low growl and then flies towards him with startling speed.

Chapter 26

Versus

Being chased by a giant, dangerous and very angry eyeball would not make most people happy, Bert however is grinning as his Lightning Boots carry him flying out of the cave, the Eye of Cthulhu close behind. Once clear of the cave entrance he changes direction quickly and leaps on top of a nearby rocky peak. The eye is swivelling around looking for him. With a soft thud Ruby lands behind him

'Bert I'm not sure what you're trying to prove but when I shout run, I mean run. I don't mean, go and make the Eye of Cthulhu mad and send him my way to join the party.'

'No, listen, I have a plan, I just need to…'

'Move!' Ruby shouts interrupting him, the large looming shape of the Brain appears behind them. She seems to have taken care of all of the floating eyeballs that previously surrounded it, but now the brain looks extra mad, and it has teeth, Bert feels sure it did not have teeth before.

Leaping into the air, Bert manages to dodge the brain. Ruby, however, jumps straight at it and at the last minute she drops and slides under it, coming out the other side; bow already drawn.

Jumping, dropping, dodging and falling, Bert does everything he can to avoid the two giant enemies. The brain seems to be only interested in attacking Ruby, the eye attacks both of them, but the two bosses ignore each other.

Eventually Bert and Ruby find themselves standing next to each other again.

'What were you saying?' Ruby asks.

'Turn. Quickly.' Bert says, out of breath.

Ruby seems surprised but does as he says. Bert pulls the arrow out from where it is currently embedded in her pack, the light on it still flashing. He loads it in his bow and notices Ruby is for once looking at him in utter confusion rather than the other way around. He does not have time to explain as the shadow of the brain is now over them. He pulls back the bow and lets the arrow fly. The arrow misses the brain and sails on past it.

'You missed!' Ruby cries, grabbing his arm ready to pull him out of the way of the approaching boss.

'No I didn't!' Bert says, pointing. Ruby looks again and sees the arrow fly behind the brain and embed itself into the eye instead. The brain pauses mid-flight, turns away from them and instead heads straight for the eye. The two bosses crash together, the eye does not seem to know what to do, but the brain keeps attacking and eventually the eye fights back. They begin smashing into each other with such great force it makes the ground shake. The fight pushes them away from Bert and Ruby whom they seem to have forgotten all about.

'How did you do *that*?' Ruby says, with something like awe in her voice.

'Just a hunch.' Bert says. He explains how he spotted the light on the arrow that was shot into her pack, how he guessed that it was like a beacon to the brain. He then realised their best chance was to get the two bosses attacking each other by firing the arrow at the eye.

Bert looks up at the fighting baddies which are now moving off into the distance. They watch as the eye lets out a roar, starts spinning wildly and when it finishes, much like the brain, seems to have grown teeth and seems to be extra angry. Bert looks at Ruby, surprised to see an eye with teeth. Ruby shrugs, clearly not surprised.

'Yeah, they do that.'

Chapter 27

Caves and Potions

They walk into the cave where the Eye of Cthulhu was leading Bert earlier, guessing that it is where they will find Maxwell.

'That was a massive risk you took back there Bert. The bosses never fight each other. That could have gone really bad.' Ruby says.

'Yeah, I guess I didn't really stop to think that I may have been making things worse. Sorry.'

'Sorry! Don't be sorry.' she says, surprised, 'It was awesome. I'm impressed, and believe me I'm not easily impressed.'

He looks down, feeling slightly embarrassed but also happy he seems to have earned some of Rubies respect.

'One question though,' she continues, 'why did you have to bring the eye out of the cave at all, it wasn't attacking us? You could have left it there, grabbed the arrow off me and shot it off into the distance to send the brain away.'

'I did think about that,' Bert says, 'but I thought whoever is controlling them would just send the eye to attack us instead. So best just to get rid of both in one go.'

Ruby nods, 'You're probably right. Once again Bert, you have impressed me.'

Bert wonders if it was more good luck than quick thinking, but does not say anything, enjoying the praise.

The cave twists and turns but heads only in one direction. Down. They do not meet any enemies, which Ruby says is completely unheard of in the Crimson Underground.

Ruby pauses after a while, listening. She then nods to herself and pulls some items from her pack. 'Here,' she whispers, giving Bert two small bottles, 'drink these.'

Bert squints to read the labels on the bottles in the dark cave. "Night Owl Potion" and "Invisibility Potion". Even Bert with his little knowledge of the game can guess what these will do.

The dark cave is suddenly much lighter thanks to the Night Owl Potion, which is useful, but more interesting by far is the fact that Bert finds he is now invisible. He cannot see his body as he looks down. He can also no longer see Ruby as she has taken the same potions. They reach the end of the tunnel and he feels Ruby tap his arm, her voice comes out of nowhere.

'Look!'

Staring ahead, Bert can see they are now facing an enormous cave. However the size of the cave is not what catches his attention and makes him freeze in fear. In the middle of the cave he can make out the head and shoulders of an enormous creature. Bert can see it is green in colour and whilst mainly human in shape, its face appears to have octopus like tentacles in place of a nose and mouth.

Chapter 28
Cthulhu

Ruby's voice whispers from the darkness next to Bert. 'I guess that's probably Cthulhu.'

Bert cannot speak, the creature is unbelievably big. Suddenly he finds the idea of the giant eye and brain far less terrifying when compared to this and would happily go back out to face them.

'I'm going to go and have a look around this place, you, well you need to keep it distracted.' Ruby says.

'How am I supposed to do that?' Bert asks, finding his voice, although it is suddenly very squeaky.

'Just, you know, talk to it, ask it some questions. You're good at that. Just wait for the invisibility potion to wear off and then pretend you're really scared of it. OK?'

'Pretend! Pretend! I don't think I'll have to do much pretending, have you seen that thing!'

There is no response from Ruby, she is gone he realises. He is by himself. He just stands there for several minutes, even after the potion has worn off, staring at the giant figure. He knows he can trust Ruby and he knows Maxwell is relying on him. But his legs do not seem to want to move.

Eventually Bert manages to convince his feet to move, he takes a shaky step forward, then another. Sooner than he would like he is at the end of tunnel, he swallows, clears his throat and speaks.

'Uh. Hello. Anyone here?'

To start with the only reply Bert hears is his own voice echoing off the cave walls, then, suddenly, a deep rumbling inhuman voice speaks, so loud the cave shakes.

'Welcome, Blazing Bert.' two large green eyes blaze to light in front of him, 'I am Cthulhu.'

Lights start blinking to life around the cave, revealing the giant sea monster he is facing. Bert gulps. 'Where is my friend? Where's Maxwell?' he calls, thinking he sounds much braver than he feels.

'Look up to your right.' Cthulhu answers.

Another torch lights up over Cthulhu's shoulder, revealing Maxwell tied to a small ledge and struggling wildly. He is shaking his head from side to side and trying to shout something through the cloth tied round his mouth.

'So I'm here. It's me you're after. You can let him go now.' Bert says.

A few moments of silence follow then the voice booms a reply, 'Perhaps. If you do as I ask.'

'And what's that?'

'I am trapped in this world Blazing Bert. A character trapped me here and only a character can release me.'

'I don't understand, what do you mean you're trapped?'

'I was made a prisoner here. I did nothing wrong but the NPCs and characters feared me as they did not understand me. So they tricked me and trapped me here, stuck forever. All I want is my freedom, you can give that to me Blazing Bert.'

'And if I help you, you will let Maxwell go?'

'That is the deal I offer you.'

Bert takes a deep breath, 'OK, OK, I agree.' he says, desperately hoping he is doing the right thing.

Chapter 29
Rescue

Bert stands there facing the monster. He is trying to figure out what to do or say next when out of the corner of his eye he notices movement, something small is flying towards him and lands by his feet. It is a shuriken and stuck to it is a hastily written note.

"Cthulhu not real. Big Robot. Keep it talking I'll get the Guide. R"

'You are making the right choice to help me Blazing Bert. Cthulhu is pleased and will reward you greatly.' the great monster's voice booms at Bert.

Bert looks the creature over more carefully. This thing is not alive, he thinks, it is a robot, a very very extremely big robot. It has been strangely still the whole time, only its eyelids moving to blink every so often. Nothing moves when it speaks to indicate a mouth. The more he looks, the more he can believe it is not alive. Bert wonders if it can even move, maybe it is just a giant blinking statue. He feels courage at this thought and speaks more boldly.

'All I want is my friend back. Tell me how this works and let's get this over with.'

'I will raise my hand out of the water, you will need to jump down to it. Stand in the circle on my palm and I will do the rest.'

Bert steps to the edge and looks down to the water far below from where the body of Cthulhu is standing, only its waist upwards visible. He wonders if it even has legs. The water begins to bubble and foam and from somewhere below a dark green shape starts rising out of the gloomy depths. A giant green scaly looking hand rises to the surface palm up. When the hand has completely emerged a green ring lights up on the palm.

Bert looks back up to the gleaming eyes and casts a quick glance to Maxwell, he tries not to show surprise as he spots Ruby is on the ledge next to him and has untied him. She must have taken another invisibility potion which has since worn off. She has lowered a rope to a tunnel below. Bert tries not to make it too obvious where he is looking and pretends to be considering Cthulhu's words. He can see Maxwell descend the rope and land in the tunnel. The Guide looks over to Bert and waves a cheery Maxwell wave. He then disappears into the dark tunnel. Ruby, still on the ledge where Maxwell had been, gives Bert a thumbs up.

Bert waits a moment to make sure Maxwell has enough time to get away and then finally speaks.

'Well thanks and everything, that sounds really good, but there's just one problem with your plan. One little problem you have not thought about.'

Cthulhu sounds amused as it speaks. 'Little problem, what little problem?'

'This little problem.' Ruby's voice cries out, in her hand she is holding a silvery blue crossbow.

To Bert's surprise Cthulhu's head spins with unnatural speed to look at where Maxwell is no longer and where Ruby is instead. She looks tiny, Bert thinks, compared to the huge monster, but she is still grinning.

'Lose something did you loooooser?'

'Noooooooooo!' Cthulhu's cry echoes around the cave making the whole space shudder.

'Eeww, you are even *more* ugly when you're mad.' Ruby adds.

The green eyes of Cthulhu start to glow brighter and brighter and all of a sudden two blazing green lasers blast out of them making a large hole in the wall where Ruby was.

Chapter 30
On the Inside

Panic grips Bert as he thinks Ruby has been fried by the lasers, however this does not last long as a flash of blue streaks across the cave and he can make her out zooming away on her Hoverboard, dodging the lasers whilst firing bright blue arrows at the giant. The green head swivels to follow her, green lasers eating into the cave wall causing it to explode into showers of rubble, but Ruby is fast and always one step ahead. Bert thinks he can actually hear her laughing.

Movement from the water below catches Bert's eye, the other immense Cthulhu hand has risen out of the water. The giant fingers on the hand are curled upwards and sparks of green light shoot between the tips forming a ball of green electricity. Ruby is so focussed on the lasers she does not see the glowing ball as the fingers uncurl and it flies towards her. Bert shouts to warn her but his voice is lost in the noise of the fight. One moment Ruby is laughing, firing arrows, the next she is hit by the electricity and is falling towards the black water below.

'No!' Bert gasps as he watches Ruby fall to the water and sink below the murky surface. In a moment of anger he leaps, his Lightning Boots propel him towards the giant green head. The face is still turned away from him, its eye lasers seem to have run out of power. Bert lands hard on top of the head.

'You have angered me Blazing Bert. I thought we had a deal. If you do not want to end up the same way as your friend, I suggest you do as I say. Come out of hiding and step on my palm. Do this and I will spare you.'

Bert realises whoever is controlling Cthulhu does not know he is on its head. The head starts moving, obviously trying to see where he has gone. Bert loses his balance, slips and falls face down. He then begins to slide along the smooth metal surface. One of his hands slips into a hand hold and he grips on tight to prevent falling. He looks to see he has actually got hold of a handle. He pulls on it and a door on top of the head opens.

Bert opens the door and pulls himself through. The inside of the giant head is how Bert would picture a spaceship. Lots of flashing lights, wires, switches and buttons. He hears the voice again, it is quieter from inside and he can hear it is accompanied by another voice. The voice of a person, a lady.

'You cannot hide from me Blazing Bert, I rule this world. I will always find you.'

Bert stands up from where he is crouched on the floor. Sat in a chair, holding a metal cup to her mouth with several wires coming out of it, is a ginger haired lady. She is tapping various buttons and pulling switches and does not see Bert approach her from behind.

'Make this easy on yourself and…'

She stops talking as Bert points Night's Edge at her. She drops the cup and raises her hands.

'Ah, there you are.' she says with a nervous laugh.

'Here I am.' agrees Bert.

'And I suppose you'll be wanting to know what's going on here...right?'

'You mean why you kidnapped one of my friends and just fried the other one with electricity. Yeah I think an explanation would be good.' Bert says feeling furious.

'Well first, let me introduce myself. I'm not Cthulhu, as you may have guessed, my name's Marshanna, Marshanna the Mechanic.'

Chapter 31

Explanations

'I'm an NPC, the NPCs in Terraria have different skills. Guide, Witch Doctor, Nurse, Goblin Tinkerer, you get the idea.' Bert listens as Marshanna starts explaining herself. 'So I'm a Mechanic. There are several of us in the game, Amy, Lauren, Korrie and so on. But just one Marshanna, one me. And I was the first Mechanic in the game, so I've always been looked up to. Anyway, life was good. All the NPCs got on well with each other and with the characters. Then one day a character turns up from outside of our Terraria. Turns out, there are millions of other Terrarias out there. Ours is just one. Can you believe it! So this character comes to us over something called the "Internet". I think it's like a teleporter. We were astounded. We thought it was just us, not that we were one of millions. So then our characters start heading off to other Terrarias over the Internet.

'You OK holding that up? Looks heavy.'

She indicates Bert's sword, his arm is aching but he does not want her to know that so he just nods.

'Where was I? Oh yes. Our characters are going to different Terrarias and are coming back with stories, apparently there are other NPCs in the other games and they have the same names as us. One day a character starts telling me, "Oh hey, I just met you in another Terraria." Another Marshanna, just like me!' She stops, waiting for a reaction, when Bert does not give one she sighs and continues more angrily.

'Listen Blazing Bert, I was important round here. The first Mechanic. How would you feel if you suddenly found out you were just a copy, one of millions?'

Bert shrugs. He does not know the answer and this does not please Marshanna.

'You're just like the rest of them. Why does nobody care? Well I do. So I tried to fix the problem. I tried to stop people using the Internet. I am the Mechanic, I can fix things. But all those other characters and NPCs start saying I don't have the right blah blah blah. So one of the more powerful characters traps me here in this world, this prison.'

'So what's that got to do with me?' Bert asks, still confused.

'Well this world has been changed so that NPCs cannot enter or leave. That's why they put me here. Only a character can get in or out. But I was here a long time, I started figuring stuff out, I built a teleporter that would take me out of here. Only problem is I need a character to make it work.'

'That's why you wanted me to stand on the green ring to make your teleporter work, so you could get out of here.'

'Exactly.'

'Ok, so why am I trapped in this world, Ruby was too?'

'Oh I figured out some other things in my long time here. I'm a good Mechanic. I managed to fix the spawn point in the game so it would grab the next passing character and trap them here. I planted lots of devices I invented all over this world. They prevent you from leaving so you're stuck like me. I also managed to find a way to control the enemies with these.' she holds up a small blinking red light. 'Turns out with nothing but time, there's a lot you can do.'

Too late, Bert realises he has lowered his sword, his aching arm giving in. Marshanna has realised it as well. Her hand darts onto the controls in front of her and presses a button, suddenly the floor under Bert slides away and he is falling through a trapdoor.

Chapter 32
Worms and Snakes

Bert falls; plunging towards the dark water below. The Lightning Boots do not fly unless he can jump first. However, as he about to hit the water something bursts from the surface, a long snake or worm like thing is suddenly smashing into him and he flies back up into the air. Still mid-air another shape collides into the side of him. Definitely a snake this time, made of bones. Great, Bert thinks.

Bert hits the wall of the cave and starts sliding down towards the water again. He manages to grab onto a jutting out rock, but he can feel his hand slipping on the wet stone. Another of the worms is heading for him. He swings Night's Edge and it smashes into the enemy but doing so he loses his grip on the rock completely and starts falling again. He lands feet first on the back of the bone snake. He takes the opportunity and jumps, the boots send him flying in the air. He aims for the tunnel he first came in through and lands inside. He can see the cave is filling up with more Giant Worms and snakes, he knows this must be Marshanna's doing.

'Not trying to escape are you Blazing Bert. I'm afraid I'm not finished with you yet.' Marshanna's voice echoes around the cave.

Bert hears a click and with an earth shuddering thump that makes him almost lose his balance a large boulder drops down from somewhere above and blocks the tunnel behind him. He is trapped. He looks over to the tunnel which Maxwell escaped through, there is also a boulder blocking that.

'There's only one way out of here for you. Step on the green circle and we will both teleport.' Marshanna starts laughing a crazy person's laugh that echoes round the cave.

Bert watches as one of the Giant Worms starts to attack the metal head of Cthulhu. The worm bashes into the face again and again, eventually going under the chin. The trapdoor that Bert fell through is still open. The worm fits through the hole and disappears inside. It is soon followed by another and another. Marshanna's laughter quickly changes to a loud scream. The door on top of Cthulhu's head is flung open and Bert can see Marshanna scrambling out firing a weapon back through the door. He can see she looks either terrified or disgusted, maybe a bit of both.

Marshanna looks over and scowls at Bert who grins back. She reaches into her pack and produces what appears to be a gold backpack that she hurriedly straps on. Flames burst from the backpack and she is in flight, propelled upwards and out of the way of a snake that was heading straight for her. The snake smashes into the door she has just climbed through and seems to get its head stuck in the process. Thrashing and wriggling the snake tries to pull free but seems completely stuck.

Bert does not have time to watch any longer as he comes under attack from a different snake and has to leap from the blocked tunnel to escape it. Bert and Marshanna fly around the cave fighting and dodging the snakes and worms, Bert with his Lightning Boots, Marshanna with her Jetpack. They both land on a low rocky ledge close to the surface of the water, out of breath Bert asks. 'I'm guessing you're responsible for this invasion, can't you stop them?'

'I can't!' she shouts, sounding furious, 'I need to get back to the controls.'

'Go in under the chin.' Bert shouts back.

'I can't. It's full of worms!'

'Out here is full of worms, what's the difference?'

'Out here I can get away from them, in there I'm trapped with them, they can touch me, and I, I, I hate worms! OK!' She spits the last words, obviously hating to admit this to Bert.

Bert has an idea. 'My Lightning Boots won't get me all the way up there in one go, give me your Jetpack and I'll fly straight up, tell me what to do when I get inside. I'll give you my Lightning Boots so you can still dodge the worms out here.'

'You think I'm gonna fall for that trick. There's no way Blazing Bert.'

'Fine, then it looks like this is game over for both of us then.'

'Aaarrgh, fine.' Marshanna, slips off her Jetpack and gives it to Bert. 'You give that back afterwards though, you hear me?'

Chapter 33
Escape Plans

With Marshanna's Jetpack strapped to his back, Bert flies up through the trapdoor under Cthulhu's chin, dodging enemies on the way. Inside the head are three Giant Worms but they cannot move easily in the small space and are no match for Night's Edge. When they are defeated, Bert shuts the trapdoor behind him. Looking up to the hatch on the ceiling he can see the head of the Bone Serpent thrashing around, completely stuck. Its mouth snapping uselessly at him. A few jabs with his sword and this too is taken care of. He quickly closes the hatch to make sure no more enemies get inside.

Bert looks at the hundreds of buttons and levers inside the robotic head. He finds two lit orange buttons and, as instructed by Marshanna, presses them. He looks through the windows that are Cthulhu's eyes and can see the enemies start to clear. She has buttons for all the enemies and a map of the world. He understands now that this is how she was controlling the Zombies and other baddies that had attacked him in such unusually large groups.

Bert has to go and face Marshanna, he will make her take the lock of the world so he can leave. He will then speak to the others, to Mike, and find out what they can do about her. But he knows he cannot leave her alone with her robot monster and all these controls, she is far too dangerous. Bert raises Night's Edge and smashes it into the control panel. It sparks and fizzes and smoke pours out of it. The lights inside the robot head start flashing red and a timer appears on the display in front of him, accompanied by a voice.

'1:00 minute until self-destruct'

'59 seconds'

'58 seconds'

Bert gulps. He did not plan on that happening. He still has no way to escape the cave. He starts pressing button and pulling levers but nothing happens.

'50 seconds'

'49 seconds'

Bert sees a lever labelled, "Eye Lasers" and the word "Charged" blinking on a display next to it. He pulls the lever.

'42 seconds'

'41 seconds'

There is a whirring noise and then the cave outside is filled with a bright green light. The lasers fire into the cave wall. Bert grabs a metal wheel in the centre of the controls and turns it. The giant robot head spins around. He lines it up with the blocked tunnel. The lasers destroy the boulder turning it to dust. He pulls the lever to turn off the lasers, pushes opens the top hatch and jumps outside.

'28 seconds'

'27 seconds'

As he flies towards the tunnel, Bert can see Marshanna heading in the same direction.

'You idiot!' the Mechanic yells, 'What have you done?'

'Let's argue later, for now let's get out of here.' Bert shouts back as they both land and start running. However at that moment there is a roar from up ahead; they both come to a standstill. In front of them and blocking the way out is the Eye of Cthulhu, obviously the winner of the fight against the brain. They are completely trapped with only seconds to go before the robot explodes.

'Any ideas?' Bert says turning to Marshanna.

'How about this!' she replies and shoves him forward towards the eye.

Chapter 34
Taking Flight

Bert stumbles forwards but manages to raise his sword at the eyeball boss. He has to try and fight it but he knows it is not a fight he can win, having already taken too much damage.

A voice behind him, a very familiar voice, shouts, 'Barney, duck!'

Bert hits the floor and a watches as hundreds of tiny blue crystal bullets sail through the air and smash into the eye. He looks up to see Ruby fly over him on her Hoverboard and land in front of him, she his holding what looks to Bert to be a mixture between a machine gun and a shark, although he wonders if he is seeing things. She is firing a constant stream of bullets into the boss and in a matter of moments the eye is giving out a final defeated roar and is no more. All that is left is a pile of items and coins on the floor.

Ruby grabs Bert's arm and she starts pulling him along on her Hoverboard away from the cave. Bert turns to see Marshanna at his shoulder. He reaches round and grabs her wrist. Marshanna yelps and suddenly the three of them are zooming through the tunnel, Ruby towing them along.

The explosion comes only seconds later. Bert turns to see the tunnel collapsing behind them. He realises with panic that they are not going fast enough to escape the falling rock, the Hoverboard is not strong enough for all three of them. He remembers he is wearing the Jetpack. He switches it on and they shoot forward with an extra burst of speed. Ruby leads them twisting and turning through caves and tunnels until they come flying out above ground.

Bert looks back to see the cave mouth collapse behind them; at the same time he feels Marshanna wriggle free of his grip and watches her drop to the ground below, instantly she is on her feet and is running. He shouts to Ruby, 'She's getting away!!' and can only watch as the Mechanic races off, the Lightning Boots giving her extra speed.

Just when it looks as if Marshanna will escape, from out of a bush Maxwell leaps and grabs her legs sending her stumbling to the floor.

Ruby and Bert catch up with Maxwell who has the struggling Marshanna pinned to the floor.

'Good to see you again Maxwell!' Bert grins to the Guide who smiles back in return.

They take Marshanna back to the Crimson hut and tie her up. They all need some time to regain lost health and to generally rest. Whilst they sit in the hut, they exchange stories.

Maxwell tells of how he was overrun by slimes whilst investigating the cave and how the King Slime trapped him inside its own body, how he saw Marshanna write the note on the cave wall, using green slime. He then got taken back to the large cave where Marshanna tied him up to use as bait for Bert.

Ruby explains what happened in the cave when she got zapped by the green electricity ball. One minute she had been fighting, the next she found herself waking up underwater, a jellyfish attacking her and her breath nearly run out. Luckily she had a Gills Potion which, as the name suggested, allowed her to breath underwater and saved her just in time, but she had fallen a long way down and had to find her way back to the surface. Eventually she made it back but only to find the cave overrun with Giant Worms and Bone Serpents.

'...and then I see the green laser blast away a boulder that was blocking the tunnel. As I'm flying up past big metal Cthulhu I hear a voice counting down, which in my experience never ends well. Then I find you and the evil Mechanic over there trapped by the Eye of Cthulhu. And, well, you know the rest. What a day!!' she says, taking a deep breath.

Bert has to agree.

Chapter 35

Departure

Bert, Ruby and Maxwell talk for some time. Marshanna sits sullenly in the corner, trying to ignore them but occasionally turning to scowl at something they say. Bert tells them what Marshanna had told him about the Internet, the other characters, and how she was trapped here.

'I forgot about that.' Ruby says. 'I was only new to the game when that happened.'

'I remember it well.' Maxwell says, looking round at Marshanna, his cheerful face looking sad for a change, 'She couldn't face knowing there was literally millions of other Marshanna's out there. She went crazy and tried to blow up all of the online worlds. She built these giant mechanical Wyverns, big dragon snake type things, that she flew around on dropping bombs and dynamite. She nearly destroyed us all.'

'She mentioned a character stopped her?' Bert asks.

'Oh yeah, Mike dealt with her.' Maxwell answered. He heard Marshanna make a growling sort of a noise on hearing the name.

'The same Mike who wrote to me?' Bert asks, Maxwell nods. Whilst some things were beginning to make sense, he still felt as if he had so many questions.

'Marshanna?' Bert asks, 'You said you needed a character to teleport you out of here. But you had Ruby already trapped in this world, why did you need me?' Marshanna does not answer, she just stares off into the distance as if she has not heard him.

Ruby says, 'Hey, do you realise he saved your life back there. He didn't have to rescue you from that explosion, most people would have left you, the least you can do is answer his question.'

'Uh! Fine.' Marshanna answers eventually, 'It's simple really, I was aware you were here,' she looks pointedly at Ruby, 'but I knew you wouldn't be easily trapped. All the enemies I sent your way you defeated without blinking an eye. No I needed someone much easier. I was hoping for another character to come looking for you, one with less fight in them, but what I got was even better, a clueless noob. Fresh to the game with no idea what he was doing. The Guide was an unexpected complication. I think because a new character always starts off with a Guide somehow he became linked to this world and could teleport even when nobody else could. I thought that was going to be a problem but actually it worked out well, I could use the Guide to get the noob to my cave. There he could teleport me and my Cthulhu out of here. Ready to get revenge. But you all managed to ruin it, my beautiful Cthulhu is gone and I won't forget it.'

'I liked her better when she was being quiet.' Ruby says and Marshanna goes back to her moody silence again.

Once they have all have had time to recover Ruby says it is time to leave; they need to get Marshanna back for the others to decide what to do with her and they also need to get Bert to the safety of the tutorial.

Ruby and Maxwell are confident that now robo-Cthulhu and all Marshanna's controls have been blown up, they should be able to leave the world without any problems. To test this Ruby grabs Marshanna and disappears.

'So, how do I do it? How do I leave?' Bert asks Maxwell.

'It's simple. All you do is close your eyes tight and think of these words. Save & Exit. You then see a whole list of worlds in front of your eyes, aim for the top one called Tutorial and when you open your eyes you'll be there. It's as easy as that.'

Bert nods, then a thought occurs to him. 'Oh, before I forget. I've got your bow.' he reaches into his pack and pulls the wooden bow out, handing it to Maxwell whose eyes light up.

'You found my bow! I remember dropping it when King Slime bought me here; when the cave collapsed I thought I'd lost it for sure. Wow, I really do owe you. Now you've saved me *and* my bow!'

'No problems, what are friends for.' Bert says. They shake hands.

Grinning, Maxwell says, 'Right, let's do this. I'll see you in the tutorial.' he then closes his eyes and vanishes. Bert takes a deep breath, squeezes his eyes shut and thinks, Save & Exit.

The End

Other books by Joe Circles:

For more Terraria Tales, try the Shambles the Face Monster series:

Follow Shambles on a journey as he turns his back on his home, the Crimson, and attempts to start a new life. Unfortunately he makes some enemies along the way, but he also makes some unexpected and unusual friends.

- **Leaving the Crimson**
- **A Guide to Danger**
- **The Slime Ninja**

For other imaginative stories, give one of my other books a go:

The Highly Unlikely Tales of Billy Fairweather 1. The Rain Dodger:

Meet Billy Fairweather and hear one of his highly unlikely tales. In The Rain Dodger Billy tells the tale of how he could do just that, dodge the rain, and how this ability is put to the test when a violent storm descends on the village he lives in. An imaginative story of odd and interesting characters and weird and wonderful events.

A Slip of the Imagination:

A vivid daydream in class and an odd conversation with his nan leads Jack Snowley to discover he has an unusual gift. He is able to visit worlds created by people's imaginations. It is on one of these visits Jack receives a mysterious note from his dad, which is strange as his dad died years ago.

Printed in Great Britain
by Amazon